When Ben Lucien Burman wrote HIGH WATER AT CATFISH BEND in 1951, he had no idea that he was writing the first of a series of books that were to become American classics, to be compared by excited reviewers with ALICE IN WONDERLAND and WIND IN THE WILLOWS, and beloved by young and old alike. Catfish Bend has now become so real to so many readers that gas-station attendants along the Mississippi between Memphis and New Orleans have been asked precise road directions to this magic land of Mr. Burman's wonderful animals.

Like Lewis Carroll's immortal classic, BLOW A WILD BUGLE FOR CATFISH BEND is at once a genial satire on the absurdities of our time, a rich entertainment that keeps the reader chuckling with every paragraph, and a thrilling adventure story. It relates how Doc Raccoon, the famous Mayor of Catfish Bend, Judge Black, the gentle vegetarian blacksnake who is trying to live down the snake's bad reputation, J. C., the sporty fox, and the others go down to Tickpaw in the marsh country below New Orleans

BLOW A WILD BUGLE FOR CATFISH BEND

to help the panic-struck animals there resist a strange and terrible invasion from the West. In the marshes we meet the sheep-dog Ironskin, banished from the Kentucky mountains because he was found with wool in his teeth; Mata, the dread lady coyote, leader of the invaders and her worshipping husband who parrots her every word; a bear who has been a wrestling bear in a circus and is always looking for someone to wrestle; and a score of other extraordinary and delightful characters in the best Catfish Bend book Mr. Burman has written.

The appeal of these unique stories is universal. While sophisticated readers were relishing the delicious subtleties of HIGH WATER AT CATFISH BEND, the New York Public Library for Children's Book Week chose it as their favorite American book of the year for young people. Over 200,000 of the Catfish Bend books are now in print.

BLOW A WILD BUGLE is one of those rare books which once read will never be forgotten; it makes the reader understand why Robert Hillyer declared Mr. Burman should have the Nobel prize.

The beguiling illustrations by Alice Caddy, the author's wife, have won universal acclaim for their subtlety and charm.

Books by Ben Lucien Burman

BLOW A WILD BUGLE FOR CATFISH BEND

THE OWL HOOTS TWICE AT CATFISH BEND

SEVEN STARS FOR CATFISH BEND

HIGH WATER AT CATFISH BEND

THREE FROM CATFISH BEND *

THE SIGN OF THE PRAYING TIGER

THE STREET OF THE LAUGHING CAMEL

THE FOUR LIVES OF MUNDY TOLLIVER

EVERYWHERE I ROAM

ROOSTER CROWS FOR A DAY

BLOW FOR A LANDING

STEAMBOAT ROUND THE BEND

MISSISSIPPI

THE GENERALS WEAR CORK HATS

IT'S A BIG CONTINENT

IT'S A BIG COUNTRY

CHILDREN OF NOAH

MIRACLE ON THE CONGO

BIG RIVER TO CROSS

* (*Omnibus volume containing the three titles above*)

Blow a Wild Bugle for Catfish Bend

Ben Lucien Burman

Illustrations by Alice Caddy

Taplinger Publishing Company · New York

For Alice Dixon Bond

Taplinger Publishing Co., Inc.
29 East Tenth Street
New York, New York 10003

Published simultaneously in the Dominion of Canada by Burns & MacEachern, Ltd., Ontario

Library of Congress Catalog Card Number 67-12429

Printed in the United States of America

The coyotes, so long found only in the West, have suddenly begun moving Eastward. Farmers have been discovering numbers of them in the wilder parts of Missouri and Illinois, and lately there have been reports of coyotes being seen in the woods of upstate New York.

Item in a New York City newspaper.

BLOW A WILD BUGLE FOR CATFISH BEND

I was sitting by the Mississippi at Catfish Bend one hot summer afternoon, thinking about the pleasant times I'd had traveling down the river on the Tennessee Belle, when all of a sudden in the willows just behind me I heard a terrible growling and snorting. A minute later two old possums burst out, having a fearful fight.

I was really shocked; this wasn't like the Catfish Bend I knew. Everything at the Bend was generally so quiet and peaceful, sometimes you could think it was heaven.

Just then my old friend Doc Raccoon came walking down the bank. He didn't look at all like his usual cheerful self, friendly and always interested in what was going on

around him. The black mask around his eyes that made him look like a bank robber was usually shiny as black velvet; now it was a dusty gray, as if he had been rolling in ashes. His eyes were worried and he'd lost a lot of weight. You could see he was terribly nervous and jumpy.

He started over to the possums to stop the fight, then suddenly changed his mind and turned away.

The possums saw him then and rushed up to him, arguing and shouting at the top of their lungs, something about one wouldn't let the other get his proper sleep.

The raccoon listened and then shook his head. "I'm sorry," he said. "But I can't let myself get involved. I've had too much trouble already."

He saw me and we walked along the water's edge a little way. I offered him one of those round candies they call jawbreakers that you suck a long time and they keep

changing color and flavor. I knew they were always his favorites. He put it in his mouth without washing it once, something raccoons never do.

Suddenly he gave a gulp and swallowed the candy whole. "You can see I'm all upset," he apologized. "That's the third unwashed thing I've eaten today."

Two crows were flying around a blackberry bush, cawing and screaming at each other over who was to eat the ripe berries. They called to the raccoon as he passed.

"I'm sorry," he said. "But I'm through interfering. You'll have to settle it yourselves."

We kept on walking and all of a sudden he gave a wild jump. "Look out!" he shouted. "It's a rattlesnake!"

I started to jump, too, and then I saw it was only a queer-shaped root. He saw it at the same time and looked unhappy. "My nerves have gone to pieces," he said. "I've been under a bad nervous strain."

I gave him the bag of jawbreakers I was carrying. "Let one melt in your mouth," I said. "Maybe it'll calm you down."

His eyes lighted. "They're too pretty to eat," he told me. He washed one in the river till it turned a bright red, then put it in his mouth. "When it's red it's the best," he said, and rolled it around with his tongue. "The red is cinnamon."

We went under a pine tree where a mother squirrel was chattering her head off, scolding her two young squirrels sitting on a branch.

"They want to stay out all night," she

called to the raccoon as he passed. "I don't know what's come over the young squirrels today. I've told them again and again it's a disgrace. But they don't even hear me. If you tell them, it might have some effect."

"I'm sorry," he said. "I can't do anything about it. From now on I'm strictly minding my own business."

I was really astonished. "I don't understand," I told him as we hurried off. "You're as different as day is from night. In the past you were always the first to straighten things out. That's certainly your reputation."

"It *was*," he answered. "But not *is*. Not after what happened. I've had enough mixing in other people's troubles. Enough for the rest of my life."

1

The raccoon began:

It all started one morning a few months ago. The sun was rising over the river, and I was just waking up when I saw it. And I sat up and rubbed my eyes, because I thought I was dreaming. It was the head of a mole, pushing out of the ground, with his funny little face and squdgy little nose all covered with mud and clay. He put a muddy paw over his mouth to tell me to keep quiet, and then motioned me to come over.

I hurried to him, still very sleepy, I guess; we'd been up most of the night opening the garbage cans at the farmer's. They'd had a big pie supper there to raise money for a new organ in the church, and it was the best garbage we'd had in years.

"What is it?" I asked.

"I'll get Byron," he answered in the high squeaky voice moles have, and he disappeared down the hole he'd been digging.

Pretty soon I saw a lot of earth being thrown up, like those big machines they call bulldozers do. And then the head of a big muskrat came out, all covered with clay,

like the mole, and then after that his whole body.

He looked all around, so scared even under the mud you could see his face was like dirty snow. And he shook so hard a lot of the earth where he was standing sort of crumbled, and he almost fell back into the hole.

"I think they're following me," he panted.

"Who?" I said, maybe a little irritated, because I still wasn't really awake. "What's the matter with you anyway?"

Instead of answering, he kept on shaking. And he shook so hard this time, the dirt where he was really gave way, and he dropped down the hole like a stone. When he came out again, a lot of dirt and mud had fallen into his eyes; he looked like he'd been baking mud pies.

The mole was out of the hole now, and he began to shake, too.

"It's the coyotes," he panted, like the muskrat.

"Where?" I asked, because I'd never seen either the mole or the muskrat before; I knew they came a long way from Catfish Bend.

"In the marshes. At Tickpaw. Below New Orleans," he answered. "Down at the mouth of the Mississippi."

"It's a terrible invasion," burst out the muskrat. "It's war."

"We've heard about all the things you've done at Catfish Bend," squeaked the mole. "So we came to get you to help us. If you don't, there's no one else. We'll all be wiped out."

"I'll call the others," I said. "Have some breakfast and then we can talk."

I went back to where we'd all been sleeping. Judge Black was up now; he was the blacksnake who'd become a vegetarian, and was always trying to live down the snake's

bad reputation. Every chance he had, he tried to show the other animals that a snake could be as gentle as a dove.

A beetle was squirming on its back, struggling to get up. Judge Black gently pushed it with his nose until it was on its feet again. The beetle thanked him and moved off.

"A good deed early is a day well begun," said Judge Black with one of the mottoes he was always using.

The talking waked J.C., the sporty fox.

He jumped up from the grass and looked around wild-eyed. "I swear I didn't steal that duck!" he shouted. "Not guilty!"

And then he realized he'd been dreaming. "I thought the farmer had me that time," he said.

The silly rabbit's nose and feet were twitching like somebody was tickling him with a straw; on his face was a foolish smile.

"I'm sorry you got me up," he said, after he'd opened his eyes. "I was dreaming I was

lost in a field of lettuce. The fence posts were carrots and the wires were sweet potato vines."

The gloomy old frog was groaning and shaking all over, having his usual nightmare seeing a snake. He waked and saw Judge Black, the blacksnake, sitting right beside him. He gave a terrified croak you could have heard up in Memphis, and then he fainted dead away. But I wasn't surprised. He'd been doing this every morning, and sometimes a couple of times a day, ever since we'd been at the Bend. I just splashed some water on him we kept handy in an old pail we called the fainting bucket, and in a minute he was sitting up again.

"It's the end of the world," he croaked. And Judge Black just looked at him very sad.

We gave the muskrat and the mole some of the things to eat we'd brought from the church pie supper, and pretty soon they were feeling better.

"I wish I had some of those carrots I dreamed about," said the rabbit, munching a leaf of lettuce.

"I dreamed about a beautiful rabbit stew," chuckled J.C., the fox, with a big wink. "Before I signed the pact here, I had rabbit stew three times a week."

The rabbit started to choke, but I was expecting it and slapped him hard on the back. Like the frog and the snake, it happened every morning.

We all sat down on a log and got ready to listen to the muskrat and the mole.

"I don't have to tell you about coyotes," said the muskrat, eating a muskmelon rind. "The Indians say the coyotes are the trickiest animals anywhere, and the Indians know us animals better than anybody in the world. Not all coyotes are outlaws, but some of them are, and a crowd of the toughest lived in the desert back of Tucson in Arizona. Things had been bad there for a long time—it hadn't rained for three years—and the outlaws heard about how fine our marshes were, full of rich muskrats and mink—our mink are the richest in the Valley. So they decided to come East and see what they could do."

"They came and they saw how wonderful and green the country was," said the mole, licking a piece of chocolate pie. "While the desert was nothing but rocks and burned clay. So after they'd robbed a few mink they decided to stay."

"They knew they weren't strong enough

to take the marshes by themselves," the muskrat went on. "So they hurried back to the desert and began puffing up all the other coyotes, young ones and old ones, good ones and bad ones, coyotes down on the plains, and coyotes up in the mountains. They told them what the Indians had said, but instead of saying the coyotes were the trickiest animals, they said the coyotes were the smartest. They were the Super Race and everybody else was inferior. They said all us marsh creatures had webbed feet like ducks, and breathed through gills like fish, and weren't real animals at all."

The mole chewed the paper plate to get the last of the pie. "They said we hopped on two feet like chickens and ate our babies," he told us. "So it was all right to take over our land. And with things being so bad in the desert, even the good coyotes believed 'em and came one night while we were sleeping. And when the sun was up,

half the animals around Tickpaw were their prisoners."

We were interrupted a minute when the little frogs of the Indian Bayou Glee Club that the old frog conducted swam over from some lily pads and asked the old frog if he wanted to lead them in morning practice as usual. But he said they'd have to wait awhile, we were busy.

The muskrat's melon rind was gone now, and he got all breathless and shivery again. "The coyotes are coming in from the West every day by the hundreds," he panted. "They're spreading all over the marshes. And now it isn't only the coyotes. They're afraid they're still not strong enough, so they're bringing in all the other desert animals they can. Wild horses, and wild steers, and Gila Monsters, and prairie dogs and tarantulas."

The last crumb of pie on the mole's paper plate was finished, and he got all shivery,

too. "They keep telling the other animals how smart the coyotes are, and if the others stay with them, they'll all be fat and rich like mink," he quavered, and his poor little blind eyes were all shiny with tears.

"They say even if they do have rain the West is too crowded," the muskrat panted again. "They say they're going to take over the marshes all the way to New Orleans."

"Even the animals that don't like water are coming," quavered the mole. "It's as if they're all hypnotized. If you don't help us before the new moon comes, there won't be a marsh animal alive . . . If you have a little more pie, I think maybe I can keep from crying."

We gave them another rind and another piece of pie. And then there was some kind of noise in the bushes, and their faces and bodies became the color of chalk.

"I knew it," panted the muskrat. "They've followed us here."

And he popped with the mole down the hole.

I looked around, but I couldn't see anything, only a crow flying through the trees, looking for something to steal. And I was pretty sure there wasn't any coyote around; it was only their imagination.

I turned to Judge Black and the others.

"We've got to go down and help," I said.

The rabbit began shivering so hard you could hear his joints crackle. "They'll kill us all," he said. "Coyotes love to eat rabbits and raccoons and foxes. Even if we escape, the wild horses will kick us to death and the bulls'll rip us to pieces."

The frog began groaning so loud each groan was like when people beat a bass drum. "The marsh animals are as bad as the coyotes," he moaned. "There's a hundred times as many alligators as here and moccasins and rattlers by the bushel. And they say there's some terrible animal, I don't know what, is the boss of them all, will kill a stranger quicker than croaking."

J.C., the fox, nodded this was so. "Let the marsh animals wash their own dishes," he said. "Besides I don't trust moles anyway. I think they just pretend to be blind to get your sympathy. Looks to me the marsh animals have sent the two of them up here for a trick. So we'll leave and they can take over the Bend."

"We're all little animals," said the rabbit. "There are just a few of us and thousands of them. What can a few little animals like us

do against coyotes and bulls and wild horses?"

The old frog began to groan again, and the little frogs of the Indian Bayou Glee Club crowded around him and looked worried. "It'd be the end of the world," he croaked. "It'd be the crack of doom."

J.C., the fox, gave a lazy yawn. "Problems. Problems," he said. "It's too early in the morning for problems." He turned to the little frogs of the Glee Club. "Let's have some music to start the day right," he said. "How about Sweet Adeline or Old Oaken Bucket?"

The silly rabbit went dancing off after a beautiful humming bird colored like a rainbow that was flying over a patch of wild honeysuckle. "O carrots and cabbage and caraway seeds!" he exclaimed. "Let's hear the music and then have a picnic."

The little frogs looked happy and got ready to sing. I stopped them before they could start.

I called the rabbit back and faced him and J.C. and the frog. I was really disgusted. "All right, we're little animals," I said. "And I know there are just a few of us. But we've got brains and ideas that have let us do big things in the past, and brains and ideas are what's important. We signed a pact to stick together and help other animals in trouble. We've got to keep our word and keep the pact and spread it everywhere we can. We can't just stand by and see these animals destroyed. We're not like some kinds of people . . . I'll go if I have to go by myself."

Judge Black, the blacksnake, who hadn't said anything yet, swallowed one of the slippery elm coughdrops he always took before making a speech, and let it slide down his long throat.

"A coward dies a thousand deaths, a hero lives forever," he said, with one of the mottoes again. "The lawful must be an example to the lawless. I'll prepare to go with you at once."

I called the mole and the muskrat from the hole where they were hiding, and when dark came, got ready to start. I was so angry with the fox and the others, I didn't even say goodbye. But Judge Black was always polite. "The only thing to fear is fear itself," he told them. "Death has many doors to let out life."

We moved down the bank, watching every shadow; the muskrat was sure we were followed. We let the mole go in front; being blind the way he was, he was the best

in the dark. All of a sudden I heard a crackling behind us, and the muskrat's long whiskers got so tight they sang, like when you don't see a fence at night and you hit one of the wires.

"It's the outlaws," he panted. "I knew they'd come. We're lost."

We crawled back in the bushes until the noise was almost right on us. And then I saw what it was; it was J.C., the fox, and behind him, the rabbit and the frog.

"The mosquitoes were bad at the Bend to-

night," said J.C. "So we thought we'd come out and get some air and walk along with you a little way."

I knew that meant he and the others were coming with us. But that's how it always was with the fox. He'd never admit he was doing anything, especially when he was doing something nice.

The frog was hopping along, out of breath and very unhappy. "The grave closes over," he croaked. "It's the day of judgment and doom." And then he added, "I hate to leave the Glee Club for so long. They'll get all out of tune."

2

It took us a couple of days, sometimes riding in an empty freight car on a train, and sometimes on a big truck. And then below New Orleans we all got on a log floating down the river and came to the marsh country at last. We guided the log toward the shore, and touched land about sunset. And I saw it wasn't anything like Catfish Bend; you wouldn't know it was the same Mississippi. As far as you could look, there was nothing but grass higher than a man's head and reeds maybe ten coon lengths tall. If there'd have been a two story house inside, you'd have had trouble seeing even the chimney.

The muskrat's wire whiskers sang again,

he was so terribly nervous. "Hide fast," he whispered. "Their spies are all over."

And this time I knew it was true.

We jumped off the logs and were into the reeds and grass quicker than a crawfish can nip your paw. We sneaked along, breaking through the reeds, and I wished we were somewhere else. Every step you took you sank almost to your waist, and when you pulled a paw out of the mud, it sounded like when people leave things behind after a picnic, and you pull the top off a bottle of pop. Fat spiders had spun webs everywhere between the reeds, and the broken webs stuck to your fur. And every once in a while a spider would come out and hiss, and say nasty things about you and your family.

The ground got solider after a little way, and we saw a tall tree, the only one around for a mile.

"We'll climb it and wait for a while," said the muskrat. "The coyotes and the others have the marsh animals surrounded. There's an old muskrat burrow goes right under the coyote camp. That's the way we came out. But we can't take a chance getting there while it's light."

We climbed the tree like he said, and in a few minutes were hidden in the branches at the top. We could see a long way now, most places nothing but reeds and grass again, with open spaces full of the big mud domes that muskrats build for their nests, and in one direction a thick cypress swamp. We looked close, and for a minute I couldn't see anything. And then a little way off I heard a funny bark, and I could make out some little brown animals looked sort of like giant squirrels. They were sitting on their hind legs, chewing grass, and barking and chattering like people.

"They're prairie dogs," said the muskrat. "They're the first ring of guards for the coyotes. If you look hard beyond them you

Chapter Two

can see some big lizards. They're the Gila Monsters people call the Tremblers. People call 'em that because just to look at 'em makes you shiver the same as if you had fever. They have terrible stomach trouble, and their breath is so bad it's deadly poison. Even without biting, if they breathe on you, it'll kill you ten feet away."

I watched them crawling along, all covered with pink and yellow spots like candy. They moved like those army tanks I saw once, that came down the road near the Bend full of soldiers. Right after the Tremblers was another line of guards, the biggest rattlesnakes you ever saw. And after them was a ring of horses, galloping and neighing and kicking stones so hard the sparks looked like their hoofs were on fire.

"They're outlaw horses," said the muskrat. "They're the special guard for the boss of the coyotes. She's a lady coyote named Mata, that's Spanish for killer. The coal black mustang is one of her assistants. They say he's kicked twenty cowboys to death."

Beyond the horses was an open place with a lot of muskrat nests—they call them muskrat colleges—I guess because muskrats are terribly dumb, and that way everybody thinks they're smart. By one of the nests, a tall cabbage palm was growing. And near it a black bull was snorting and pawing the earth, kicking up so much dust the grass around him seemed smoking.

"He's Mata's other assistant," said the muskrat. "He's an outlaw bull ran away from one of those big ranches in Texas. They say his father was a fighting bull in Mexico. There's a price of five thousand dollars on his head."

Something started to come out of the muskrat nest by the cabbage palm now, and everybody around it got quiet. And the wild horses and the bull stood waiting, like they were expecting a queen. And then out walked a small yellow lady coyote, and after her a coyote so big and shaggy he looked almost like a wolf.

The muskrat's whiskers sang like a whole wire fence when a hurricane is blowing; his legs shook so and got so like rubber, I was afraid he was going to fall down. "It's Mata," he said. "The big fellow's her husband. He thinks he's the leader, but he's dumb as us muskrats. But she makes up for everything. She's the smartest and the wickedest coyote in the world."

The two coyotes and the bull moved up to a high mud wall that'd once been what

they call a levee around a house and a garden to keep out the floods. Only now there was nothing but a few foundation stones and a broken fence; the house and the garden were gone. The wild horse came up to join the two coyotes and the bull, and polished his hoofs in some sand. And the bull sharpened his horns on a rock and they all started walking around the wall. They howled and roared and pawed and neighed; and the horse kicked at a little tree that got in his way, and it went up in the air like a kite. I could see they were trying to scare somebody.

"The wall is around the camp of the marsh animals," said the mole. "They're all down in muskrat holes and won't come out till night. They're all that are left. The others have been taken prisoners or run away. When they're gone, it's the finish."

It got dark soon after that and we climbed down the tree and saw a big muskrat hole. And we went down inside, and the mole took the lead again, and we followed close behind him. I hate holes in the ground myself, and this was a long one. But now and then the muskrats had glowworms in the ceiling, so it wasn't as dark as I thought. Here and there toadstools were growing, and every once in a while the rabbit would pick one up and smell it, hoping maybe it was a carrot.

We went on and on.

"I don't trust this muskrat," J.C. whispered to me. "We've been walking through these tunnels long enough to be in Mexico."

J.C. being J.C. was always terribly suspicious.

All of a sudden there was a rumbling overhead, and I knew we were under the camp of the outlaws. And by the glowworm light I saw the mole stop and put his ear to the side of the burrow to listen. Being blind a mole can hear better than anybody.

"There are a lot of new animals," he said, and his voice was all shaky again. "They must be getting ready to attack. I'm happy now that I am blind. Because then I won't be able to see the terrible things that are going to happen."

We went on a little way, and then I heard a kind of moaning.

Chapter Two

"We're under the outlaws' prison camp," said the muskrat. "It's where they keep some of the marsh animals they've captured. It breaks my heart when I pass here. I've a lot of friends and relatives up there. A brother-in-law and a nephew and several first cousins. We muskrats are great family animals, you know."

We neared the end of the tunnel, I could tell by the moonlight coming in, and I heard a terrible yelling and screaming and cursing.

"It's our camp," said the mole. "That's Ironskin. He's having a trial."

I wondered who Ironskin was, but I didn't think it was the time to ask.

We came out of the tunnel now, and the moon was so bright I could see almost like day. A dog was sitting on a stone, a shaggy dog with an enormous head and paws and body, almost as big as a Great Dane. He was yelling and screaming at two otters standing before him, and both otters smelled strongly of fish.

"It's Ironskin," said the muskrat. "They call him that because he's got eighteen bullets in his sides."

"He used to be a sheepdog up in the Kentucky Mountains," said the mole. "The sheriffs caught him with wool in his teeth from killing a sheep, and they put him in jail, and sentenced him to be shot. But he escaped and came down here to the marshes a couple of years ago, and the marsh animals made him the boss."

One of the otters, an old fellow with gray patches where he'd lost his fur, mumbled something about the law.

Ironskin's eyes got wild. He ground his big teeth and started yelling and screaming again. "Law! Law! Don't talk to me about the law! I'm an escaped convict, so I know the law! A convict knows the law better than anybody else, don't he? He broke it!"

The younger otter started arguing, something about a catfish he'd caught, and the older one began arguing against him.

Ironskin stopped them in the middle. "Fight it out!" he screamed.

The muskrat's eyes got terribly sad. "He comes from the feud part of Kentucky where the people were always shooting each other. Fighting is the only thing he knows."

"They fight and then it starts a blood feud," said the mole. "And then they keep fighting for years and years."

Judge Black looked like a thunder cloud. "Use a leaky churn and you'll have no butter," he said. "It's a shocking way to conduct a trial."

As he spoke the two otters began biting and clawing each other. And in a minute all the animals that were sitting around, possums, and ferrets, and mink, and muskrats began battling, too. They kept it up, almost tearing each other to pieces, until they were all worn out.

"Next case!" screamed Ironskin.

This time a muskrat came forward, and behind him came a big possum. The muskrat told Ironskin the possum didn't have any place to stay, and the muskrat let him in his burrow for one night. But the one night became a week, and the week became two months, and the possum had eaten all the food the muskrat had saved up for a year. And besides, he'd fall asleep in the entrance of the burrow, and being a possum that slept so hard, nobody could wake him up.

"Fight it out!" screamed Ironskin, and they and all the other animals started to claw and bite just like they did before.

The noise got the coyotes and the animals

on the other side of the wall all excited. And they began to howl and carry on like they were crazy. And when I thought how they were just waiting to pounce, I couldn't stand it any longer.

I jumped in front of the muskrat and the possum where they were rolling on the ground.

"Stop!" I shouted.

Everybody jumped like I'd fired a cannon. They all stopped quarreling and looked at me like I'd dropped out of the moon. All except Ironskin, and he glared at me with his dog's eyes all red, and he gnashed his teeth so loud it sounded like hail.

"Who are you?" he yelled.

I answered him in a voice soft as milk. "I'm the raccoon in charge at Catfish Bend," I said. "You sent for me."

The red left his eyes, and his face got friendly, and all the others got the same. But funny thing when he talked, he was so used to snarling and growling he couldn't talk any other way.

"I'm sorry," he snarled, giving me a nice smile. "I apologize. It's been a bad day."

I introduced Judge Black and the others to him and the marsh animals, and then I told them what I thought. "It's madness to be fighting each other this way," I said. "Fighting is the stupidest thing in the world." And I told them about the pact the animals at Catfish had signed in the big flood, how they'd found out they couldn't stay alive if they kept on quarreling and promised to stick together always and not fight any more. "The way I've heard, if you hadn't been fighting so much, the outlaws could never have come. Now if you're ever going to drive them out, you've got to work together like brothers."

"Divided we are broken by the breath of a fly," said Judge Black. "United we withstand the hurricane."

"I'm sorry," Ironskin snarled again, looking very humble. "It's the way I was raised. I don't know any better."

Most of the marsh animals went off to sleep, and we sat down with Ironskin and began talking over our plans. We'd been talking only a minute when I saw he was terribly jumpy. Every once in a while he'd leap to his feet and shout "Fight it out!" to the empty air, and then he'd apologize again.

"I'm going to pieces being cooped up for weeks in the little space inside this wall," he said. "Every minute the coyotes and the other outlaws are doing something to us. My spies, the ferrets, came in a while ago and told me they're getting ready for the final attack. They say it'll certainly be in a few days. It may come any minute."

I saw why he was so jumpy when after a little while a big diamond-back rattler from Arizona came out of a hole in the

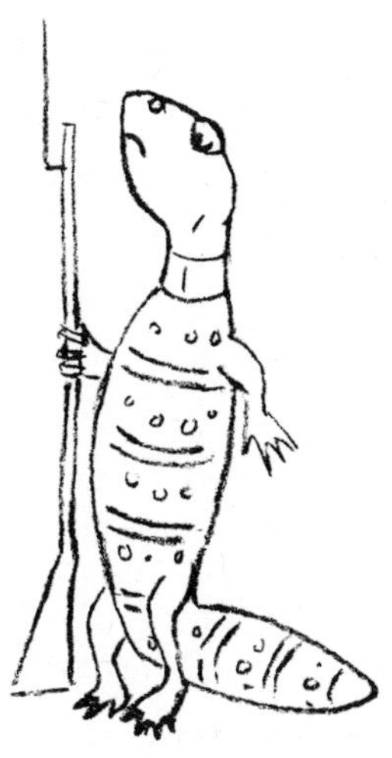

corner and then headed straight for him. But Judge Black saw him just in time, and raced between the snake and the dog, and stood there hissing and looking awful. Though the Judge is usually so gentle, the other snakes know if he wants to he can be a terror. And the rattler called him a nasty name, and got out again in a hurry. A few minutes later the mole whispered to me he heard something crawling across the ground. And I looked and right in back of Ironskin was a Gila Monster, just getting ready to breathe on him. I was going to jump at the Trembler, but J.C. was faster. But the Gila was too far off and raced to the hole he came through.

"I'd have finished him," said J.C. "But he gave me a pitiful look that made me think of my mother and I let him get away. That's the trouble with me. I'm too tender-hearted."

You could be sure no matter what happened, J.C. always had an excuse.

Ironskin was dripping with sweat, and it wasn't a hot night, either. "Those Gila Monsters are too much," he snarled. "I have to do something to quiet my nerves. If I don't, I'll go crazy."

He called to a skinny old hound dog that was sleeping by the wall, and a minute later the hound came over and sat down at his side. He gave the hound a nervous smile. "Sing me a mountain song, Anse," he growled. "You know. One of the good old-timey kind."

"Anse came with him from the mountains when he escaped," whispered the mole. "When Anse sings him a mountain song, it quiets his nerves quicker than anything."

Anse threw back his skinny head and began to whine out a song, something about the Foggy Dew. His voice was awful, and I could see the frog was covering his ears; running the Glee Club he was used to fine music. But it did funny things to Ironskin. His eyes filled with tears; and pretty soon his whole body was shaking with sobs.

"I can't help it," he wept, and now he wasn't snarling. "It does it to me every time I hear mountain music. It makes me think of my happy life there before they branded me a murderer."

He choked back his tears. "I didn't kill

that sheep. Somebody else was the real criminal. The wool in my mouth came from a lamb that was drowning in the creek and I pulled him out. I was really a hero, not a villain. I'm a noble dog, from one of the first American dog families. There's a monument to a great great grandfather of mine who's buried in the Arlington cemetery in Washington. He saved a whole company of soldiers in France in the First World War. And now I've come to this, an escaped convict hiding out in these terrible marshes. I'd give my life to get back to my friends and my family. But I'll never see my mountains again."

I tried to cheer him up. "You never can tell," I said. "Maybe things'll change."

Judge Black nodded. "The only thing in this world which is permanent is change," he said.

Pretty soon Ironskin was fine again and snarling at everybody like he did before. And we began talking about our plans where we'd left off.

"It's a wonderful thing you've come," he growled. "Everything'll be different now. We'll send out messengers to all the animals hiding in the marshes to get ready. And then we'll attack the outlaws here, while they think we're finished. We'll sweep them off the face of the earth."

He rushed around, barking out commands, and waking up the snake doctor, so he could look over everybody to see they were in good shape. And then he told some muskrats to begin digging holes under the dirt wall around us, so we could come out in the outlaws' camp and take them by surprise. And everybody was excited and happy, now they knew they were going to win.

And then all of a sudden I heard a fearful sound on the other side of the wall, a howl like the wind in a tornado.

"It's the coyotes!" cried the muskrat. "The outlaws are attacking!"

And then everything went black.

3

When I came to I could tell it was almost morning. It was just beginning to get light. My body felt funny, and I tried to move, and right away I knew I couldn't. And then I saw I was all tied up with vines, the way men tie up a pig. I looked around now and I could see I was in a kind of cave, with straw and reeds scattered everywhere; it was another muskrat nest. And lying on the straw were Ironskin and my four friends from Catfish Bend, all tied up like me. Outside the entrance was a giant Gila Monster, standing guard, and after him a couple of big rattlers, coiled up and ready to strike.

The other animals in the cave were waking up, too, and I was going to say something to the rabbit who was next to me, when there was a lot of noise outside, and I saw the Gila Monster salute. And then Mata, the lady coyote, came in, and her husband that looked like a wolf was with her. I had a chance to see them both plainly now; they passed very close. Mata's body was pretty skinny—they said she was one of those animals that eats all the time, but never gets fat. Around her neck was a strip of white fur, the way coyotes sometimes have, that looked like a fancy collar; and her yellow hair was all slicked back, so it looked like it was pasted down with oil. Every once in a while she'd turn and smooth down some loose hairs with her tongue. You could see right away she was the kind of animal that watches her looks every minute. But it was her eyes that shocked you; they were the cruelest eyes you ever saw in your life, green with red flashes showing in back, like they were green glass

somebody was trying to set on fire. Her husband was nothing but heavy muscle and bone, with sort of dull eyes and a droopy mouth; like the muskrat had said, you could tell he was terribly stupid.

Mata moved to the middle of the cave and waited until she could see everybody was awake.

"I'm Mata," she snapped, and her voice cut like when you step on a knife. "I guess you know that means The Killer. There's no use your trying to escape. You can see the Gila Monster and the rattlers for yourself. And there are plenty of others."

Her dumb husband nodded his head like a donkey. "You can see for yourself," he said. "Plenty of others."

Mata looked around at each of us out of her cruel eyes. "I'm going to what they call brainwash you all," she said with a sneer. "When I get through each of you will say exactly what I want you to say. Exactly what I want you to do."

"Exactly what she wants you to say," grumbled her husband. "Exactly what she wants you to do."

The rabbit's face got red as a beet, and it looked like he was going to burst. I thought at first he'd swallowed a piece of lettuce wrong, but he was choking with fright.

"She's telling the truth," he managed to whisper between chokes. "Coyotes can hypnotize you better than snakes. I've heard it plenty of times from animals that have been out West. They do it by wobbling their eyes. It's the way coyotes catch rabbits."

"A toad came to the Bend from Oklahoma once," groaned the frog. "He said the Indians were always worried when the coyotes were around. They were afraid the coyotes would hypnotize their children and run off with them into the desert."

Mata and her husband went out now, and I saw them walk off with the mustang and the bull who'd been waiting by the entrance.

A couple of big coyotes came in then and took Ironskin away. In a few minutes they brought him back, still tied like a pig, and threw him down in a corner. His face was like stone and his eyes were all glassy; I could see he was hypnotized. "Coyotes are brave. Coyotes are wonderful," he said, and his voice was changed, all high and squeaky like the mole. "I love coyotes more

than anything in the world." And he said it over and over.

Next they took off the frog and the rabbit and brought them back fast, and they began talking like Ironskin, too.

"No coyote'll hypnotize me," said J.C. "I know a few tricks. I wasn't born yesterday."

But they carried him off, and in maybe

an hour they brought him back, and he was just the same as the rest.

Judge Black took a couple of hours, but I wasn't surprised. He was a fine hypnotist himself.

It was awful to hear them saying the words over and over all together, like the people I saw praying in a church one time when I went up an apple tree there to pick the preacher's ripe apples so the others would grow better. "Coyotes are brave. Coyotes are wonderful," the animals said. "If everybody was like a coyote, this would be a wonderful world."

Now only one animal was left, and that animal was me. And they carried me off to a smaller burrow where Mata was sitting, waiting. And she stared at me, and the flashes in her eyes got brighter, until they were like a fire showing through ice. And then her eyes started getting bigger and bigger, and pretty soon melted into a single eye,

big as the center of a sunflower. And all of a sudden the big eye began to wobble like those yo-yo balls children have on a string. And then it began spinning around, all full of sparks, like the pinwheels they have on the Fourth of July. And all the time Mata was talking low, almost like she was singing.

I felt myself getting sleepier and sleepier, but I managed to fight the sleepiness off. All the rest of the day she tried, but I was still awake, and I could see she was getting worried.

"These raccoons are always tricky," she said to her husband beside her. "I'll leave him here and come back tonight. Sometimes it works better in the dark."

"Better in the dark," said her husband.

They went outside, and night fell fast, and before I knew it she was back, with the big eye wobbling and spinning again. And this time I felt myself getting sleepier and sleepier, and felt my own eyes closing. And then I sort of heard myself saying, "I dearly love all coyotes. I wish I had nine lives like a cat, so I could give them all for a coyote."

And I don't know anything after that.

How long I was that way I don't know; I think it was all that night and all the next day. Anyway, it was night again when I woke up with a terrible aching in my head, like the time the limb of a tree I was sitting on broke in a storm. And then I saw I was back in the big burrow with Judge Black and J.C. and the others mumbling over and over about the coyotes, and then I remembered what happened.

I looked out through the entrance of the burrow now, and in the moonlight I could see the Gila Monster still guarding. Beyond him a lot of coyotes were standing around in a circle, and at first I didn't know what they were doing. And then one coyote got out in the middle and threw back his head, and began to howl like he was dying. And then I knew he was doing what I'd heard coyotes always do; he was howling at the moon. Pretty soon more coyotes joined him, and then more and more; and then Mata and her husband howled, too. There were mournful howls that sounded like a cow mooing for her calf; and terrible howls like a screech owl when an animal ghost comes around. The coyotes all started running in a circle, howling louder and louder. And the other outlaws stood watching, as if they wanted to run, too.

They got tired of howling after a while, and then Mata began to make a speech. And the animals gathered around and listened, and I knew then why they did whatever she said. I kept myself from looking at her eyes; I knew what looking would mean. But even then just listening to her voice was like a terrible magnet pulling you closer and closer. And pretty soon a lot of the animals were the way I had been; they were hyp-

notized. She began talking louder and faster, never even stopping for breath. And then I knew if I was going to do something, now was my only chance.

I began struggling and biting at the vines that bound me; they'd gotten dry and were easy to cut through. And I hurried to the fox and cut him loose first; I knew he'd be the easiest to wake.

I shook him hard, and he started to say something about coyotes, so I shook him harder. And all of a sudden he jumped to his feet. "Heads down!" he shouted. "The farmer's after us with a gun!" And a second later he was laying flat on the ground. I guess he thought he was back in his old days stealing a chicken, so I knew he was himself again.

I told him fast what'd been going on and then we cut the others loose, too. It was easy to wake Judge Black, but we couldn't wake the frog or the rabbit, and Ironskin was the same way. I'd noticed the ground where I was standing sounded hollow, and I figured it was a muskrat tunnel under us. And the fox and I kept one eye on the Gila and began to dig, and pretty soon we'd dug through. I knew these tunnels were all connected, and I thought that way we could get out to where we'd come in. The fox picked up the rabbit, and Judge Black carried the frog. And I got Ironskin to his feet, and pulled him along in his sleep.

We let Judge Black go down first; he was used to holes, being a snake. We went right

under where Mata was making the speech, and after a while we saw moonlight. We didn't know just where we were, but we thought we'd better come out anyway. We were climbing out one by one, when I heard the rabbit give a terrible cry. And then I knew he'd waked up and found he was being carried by a fox. And then the frog gave a terrible groan, and croaked "Crack O' Doom," and I knew he'd waked up, too, and saw he was being carried by a snake.

We'd come out on a grassy little island in the marsh, with a narrow bayou running all around; we decided to stop and pitched our camp by a clump of palmettos. An island was the best place we could find; most of the outlaws, being desert animals, couldn't swim and were afraid of water. We shook the dirt from our fur and skins and held a council of war.

"This is too big for us to handle alone," I said. "As soon as it's light, we'll scatter and see what we can find. We've got to get help somewhere."

The sun came up and Ironskin jumped to his feet. "Fight it out!" he snarled, and I thought he was going to be all right. But his voice was terribly queer, the way it was before. And when I looked at his eyes, I saw he was still hypnotized.

We put down a log over the bayou for a bridge and four of us started out, each in a different direction. The rabbit stayed behind to watch the camp and look after Ironskin.

I didn't see anything at first, and then in the cypress swamp not far off, I heard a terrible growling and roaring. And I crawled through the weeds and tangled brush until I found the reason. It was a bunch of bears from that part of the country, having a meeting the way they do in the Spring and

the Fall. They have a good time and talk things over, how to dig under the new electric fences people put around bee hives to keep the bears from stealing the honey, or maybe thinking up some new trick to make hunters shoot themselves.

They were all gathered around one of those mounds of earth they say were built by the Indians. One side had fallen away, so it made a dirt cliff almost as high as a steamboat. And everywhere in the cliff were little caves that you could see were full of honey. It was like what they call the bee bluffs farther north, where the bees have been putting their honey away longer than anybody can remember. There were maybe a hundred bears, I guess, and they'd sit and talk, and then one of them would get hungry. And he'd climb one of the dead cypress trunks standing alongside the mound and grab a big chunk of honeycomb, and then he'd bring it down. Bears always have their meetings at a bee bluff whenever they can.

I'm not afraid of bears; they say bears and raccoons are cousins. So I went right up and talked to a little cinnamon bear that was nibbling at a crab apple.

"You'll have to talk to that fellow over there," he said, and he pointed to a big black bear talking to a crowd a little way off. "He's the boss. He used to be a wrestling bear in a circus."

I waited while the big bear went on talking. I didn't want to interrupt. And every now and then he'd wave his paws, motioning the other bears to come to him, and call out, "Anybody here want to wrestle?"

He'd been trained that way in the circus.

I walked up to him when he was through his speech.

"You want to wrestle?" he asked.

I asked if he and the other bears would help us.

He shook his shaggy head. "We're not

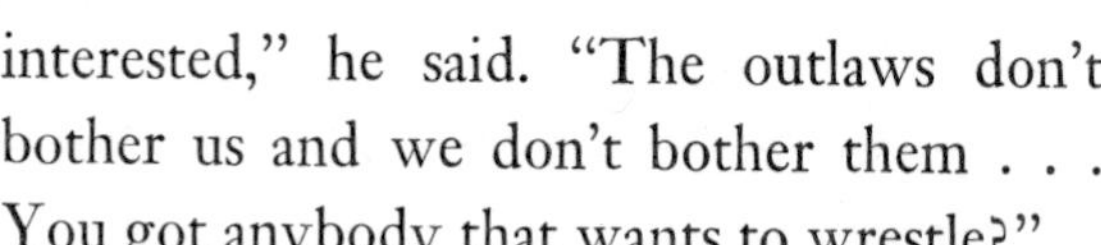

interested," he said. "The outlaws don't bother us and we don't bother them . . . You got anybody that wants to wrestle?"

I walked off feeling bad. And then I had an idea.

I've had a lot of experience with bees; honey is a raccoon's business. A bee line that people talk about isn't straight at all. That's just another of the things people get all mixed up. A bee line winds around every which way; a bee loaded with honey wants to throw anybody following off the track; there are so many thieves around. But I watched where the paths of the bees crossed, and I knew that would be the big hive where the queen would be staying.

I found it a little way from the mound in an old cypress tree that'd been struck by lightning. I climbed up and on the way met a couple of old bees sitting on a dead branch, fanning themselves and breathing hard. I could see they were all worn out. I asked

them if the queen was there.

"She is and I wish she wasn't," said the older bee. "She's a new queen came in from around New Orleans and she's driving us crazy. The people there have been experimenting with bees, and they've mixed 'em up with lightning bugs, so they work day and night. We used to have a nice life here, but now we never get any rest."

"I'm so tired I can hardly stand up," said

the other bee. "It's bad enough bees being part lightning bug. But they made a mistake and got this queen all mixed up with a tumble bug. When you try to talk to her she makes you dizzy."

I climbed on up and found the queen in the hive, sitting before a big honeycomb.

"Pardon me while I tumble," she said, very polite, and did a somersault.

I told her my plan, and all the while the light inside her was flashing on and off, and every once in a while she'd do a somersault again. Like the bee on the branch said, it made you terribly nervous.

She listened, but then she shook her head. "I can't do it," she told me. "The other bees would get rid of me right away if I did. My position as queen is very shaky here . . . Pardon me while I tumble."

I climbed down the tree and decided; if the bees wouldn't give me the honey I needed, I'd have to take it myself.

I rolled myself in mud, the way raccoons always do before they rob a hive, and went up the tree again. This time a lot of bees came out to sting me, but covered with mud the way I was they couldn't hurt me at all. I broke off a chunk of honey as big as I could carry, and scrambled down, and hurried off toward our camp on the island. When I got there, I was happy to see the mole and the muskrat talking to the rabbit. Being underground animals and used to getting away in holes, they'd never been captured at all. The fox and Judge Black came in toward sunset. They hadn't seen very much, only some muskrats and other marsh animals hiding out like ourselves.

I told them what I planned, and as soon as it was dark I went off with the muskrat and the mole, and we were away a couple of hours.

In the morning we left the muskrat to look after Ironskin and hurried off to the honey mound. And then we climbed a big tree by it, and watched and waited.

"I don't think it'll work," said J.C., after we'd been there a little while. "That Mata will know right away it's a trick. She's almost as smart as a fox."

What I'd done was very simple. I knew that coyotes were as crazy as bears about honey; we'd made a honey trail all the way from the outlaws' camp to the Indian mound. If Mata and the other outlaws came there to get the honey, I was sure the bears would go wild and drive them away.

It got later and later, and the buzzards started circling, looking for their lunch, and still there was no sign of anything.

Judge Black took a coughdrop. "A watched pot never boils," he said.

4

He'd hardly spoken when we saw Mata and her husband come racing, licking up the trail of honey as they ran. And behind them came the mustang and the bull and a lot of the other outlaws, sniffing the ground to find out if any was left.

"It's a bee bluff!" shouted Mata as she saw the mound, and they all started charging forward, howling and neighing like animals that have gone wild after sleeping too long under the moon. Just that second the bears came back; they'd been off in the swamp where a bear from Georgia was showing them a new way to tell when peaches were ripe. And they saw the outlaws swooping down on the honey, and then the battle began. It was a terrible battle, with bears and coyotes and wild bulls and horses all tangled up and charging in every direction.

J.C., the fox, was laughing so hard he almost fell out of the tree. "That was a wonderful trick of mine," he said. "I knew it couldn't fail."

Course I didn't say a word. It was just J.C. all over.

They fought till dark and the moon came up, and still they didn't stop. And then we heard the coyotes go howling off into the distance.

"The bears have won," said Judge Black. "If night falls, day must come at last. The marsh animals are saved."

"I'll write a poem about it," giggled the rabbit—he was always writing poems:

"The coyotes came for the honey.
Honey to a coyote is better than money.
But—"

We didn't let him finish. The rabbit's poems were always so bad they gave you stomach ache.

We stayed up in the tree all night, feeling very happy. We didn't leave because we heard funny noises under us, and we figured the bears were prowling around, watching for any outlaws coming back. That way they'd be very nervous, and a nervous bear

isn't butter. With the first light we started down, and we got a terrible shock. And a second later we were up in the tree again. Somebody was prowling under us all right. But it was Mata and the outlaws. The coyote howling we'd heard wasn't defeat; it was a cry of victory. It shows the trouble that can come when you don't know the other animal's language.

Near Mata the big bear that'd been the wrestler in the circus was standing with his eyes like they were white marbles and his body like it was iron. And all the time he was mumbling over and over, "Coyotes are wonderful. Coyotes are the Super Race." He was just the way it'd been with us.

And then he and the other bears began going to the bee mound and collecting the honey. This time they didn't climb the cypress trunks. Instead they went straight up the sides of the mound. And it was so steep and dangerous, each trip they were risking their lives. And they'd bring the honey to Mata and lay it in a pile. And Mata and her husband and the mustang and the bull would stuff and gorge; if any of the others would come around, the mustang would let go with his hoofs and growl, "Get away or I'll kick you to death. The way I did the forty-eight cowboys."

All day the bears climbed like what they call zombies, gathering the honey, and adding to the pile. And plenty of times some of them fell. It was a pitiful thing to see. By night they had it all, and Mata and the others wrapped chunks of it in leaves, and carried it off to their camp. And we came down from our tree and went back to our island; we walked like our best friends had just died.

"We might as well go back to Catfish Bend," said J.C. "The bear's the biggest animal here. If the bears can't beat them, nobody can."

Chapter Four

"The grave closes over," croaked the frog. "We're dead as dust."

"The night is dark again," said Judge Black. "We are in encircling gloom."

And when Judge Black said something like that you knew things were really terrible.

The rabbit brought out some wild strawberries he'd found, and strawberries were our favorite. But we felt so bad nobody ate one; we let them go to the ants.

We were sitting there, not saying a word,

when we heard a crackling in the palmetto on the other side of the bayou. And then we saw it was a big Brahma bull, you know, one of those bulls with a hump that came from India way back. Even in the moonlight his big eyes like a deer were so sad and he looked so miserable, we could tell he hadn't come to hurt anybody.

"I've left the coyotes," he said, when we'd let him come across. "I was part of the herd of bulls that came with them out of the West. I was born on a ranch in the same part of the desert as Mata, back in Arizona. And now I've left them, and they're all the friends I've ever had."

I asked him why and his big eyes got sadder. "I have nightmares," he said. "My brother disappeared one night, when I was a young calf, and nobody knew what happened. I've been looking and searching for him from that night on, and I've had bad dreams ever since. When I have nightmares

I scream out and it always starts a stampede. The last stampede I started in Arizona thirty-three cattle were hurt . . . But that wasn't the reason I left."

I shook the ants off the strawberries and offered him some; he pushed them away.

"There were plenty who wanted me to go," he said. "But plenty who wanted me to stay. A Brahma bull's terrible in a battle. But last night I'd eaten too much green grass, and I woke up and heard Mata and her husband talking; they didn't know I was listening. And then I learned what happened that night to my brother. I needn't look for him any more. He hurt his leg going down a mountain and met Mata and her husband and asked them for help. And instead they—"

He couldn't finish the sentence, he got all choked up. But he didn't have to say anything else. I knew the habits of coyote outlaws.

He got hold of himself and went on talking. "I didn't sleep any more after that, and got away as soon as I could. I didn't want to breathe the same air as those two horrible animals." His face got fierce, and he pawed the ground like the wild bull and tossed his horns and bellowed. "We Brahma bulls are like elephants. We never forget. Now all I want is to avenge my brother's death and join the coyotes' enemies. I was

 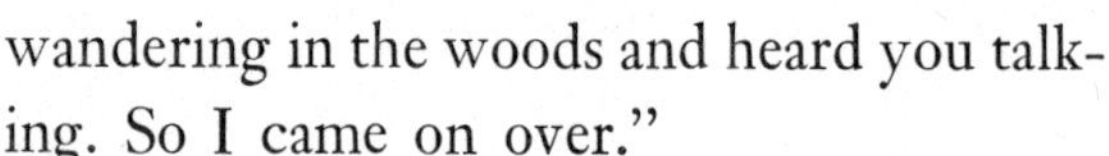

wandering in the woods and heard you talking. So I came on over."

We said he was welcome and thought he might be hungry now and offered him the strawberries again.

"I can't eat fruit," he said. "Only grass and not much of that. I have a nervous stomach. I've had it ever since the night my brother was lost."

He was quiet a minute and I could tell he was thinking. "I see you're going to be my friends," he said. "I ought to let you know what Mata and her gang are planning. They're going to drive out every animal like you along the Mississippi—all the way from near Canada, where it starts, to down here at the Gulf of Mexico. They're going to bring in more and more animals from the West and take over the whole Mississippi Valley."

He pushed the strawberries farther away. I guess it bothered his stomach. "They're not only going to make you Mississippi animals leave. They're going to drive you all the way out to the desert. Only yesterday I heard Mata laugh and say it'll be good for your health for you and them to trade places. She says people go out to the desert for their health and with animals it'll be the same. But I know what it'd mean. It's all right for the coyotes and the others and me with my Hindu blood. But in those hot rocks and that hot sand, you'd be dead in a couple of hours."

For a long time after he finished we sat so quiet if a spider web had fallen it would have sounded like thunder. We'd known some dreadful times, floods, and forest fires, and the year when the hunters took over the Bend. But this was the worst thing that had happened in the world since we had been born.

The rabbit began to whimper. Then he got up and started walking.

"Where you going?" I asked.

"I'm going back to Catfish Bend," he said. "That way when they kill me I'll die in a place where I'm happy."

The frog got up, too. "The grave closes over," he croaked. "I'm going with him."

I stood up and blocked their path. "You're crazy," I said. "It won't do any good to run away. These animals are outlaws who'll destroy our pact and set animals against each other everywhere. There'll never be any more peace. They'll never be satisfied. After they take over the Mississippi, they'll want to take over the whole country. We've got to stay here and stop them before they destroy the world."

Judge Black nodded. "He who turns and runs away will live to battle another day," and then he looked worried. "No. No. That's the wrong motto. The coward who runs away will never more see a sunny day."

Ironskin, who'd been lying on the ground like a log, jumped up all of a sudden. "Fight it out!" he snarled. And this time for a minute his voice sounded natural. And then like the hound had done, he started singing Foggy Dew. And his voice was high and squeaky again. And I knew he was still a zombie.

We sat with the Brahma bull talking over what we could do. And then off in the distance there was a noise like a storm, and we went to see what it was, and when I saw I shivered. In the moonlight across the marsh, as far as you could look, the animals were marching in from the West; coyotes and wild horses, and wild bulls and cows, and rattlers and Gilas and scorpions. And I could see they were believing more and more the stories Mata was telling them about how terrible the marsh animals were and how the coyotes were so wonderful. Plenty of them had glassy eyes and moved like they were walking in their sleep; like the animals when Mata made the speech, they were hypnotized. And they kept murmuring like the wind, "Coyotes are the Super Race."

It's almost as easy to hypnotize some animals as it is to hypnotize people. Judge Black told me he knew a snake that could hypnotize thirteen birds at once. But the Judge got him to sign the pact and now he's a vegetarian, too.

"We've got to act quickly," I said, when we were back at our camp. "By morning they'll find out where we are. With all these animals, they'll attack right away. We've got to attack them first."

Judge Black nodded again. "The best defense is offense," he said.

We decided to send a messenger up the river to tell the animals what was happening, and ask them to send help. And we decided J.C. would be the best to go; he was a fine persuader, and with all the training foxes had in hunts he could run terribly fast.

We loaded him up with berries and some paw-paws we found so he wouldn't go hungry. And just before sun-up he stepped onto the log to start out, and we all had lumps in our throats. He was a rascal, J.C., but we all felt he was really a friend.

He gave the rabbit a big wink and pretended to look hungry. "Take care of yourself," he said. "If not for yourself, for my sake."

And he gave the rabbit another big wink, and laughed, and then he waved goodbye and was gone.

5

Like I thought, soon after sunup the outlaws found our camp; they'd missed the Brahma and followed his trail. On the other side of the bayou now there was a line of rattlers near the water's edge, with the Gila Monsters in back. But it didn't make too much difference so far; as long as the muskrat tunnel was right by us, we could drop down into it and go almost anywhere we liked.

A couple of days passed without much happening. And I stayed awake most of each night trying to think what we could do, and wondering if J.C. had gotten through.

All the time we kept trying to wake

Ironskin, slapping him on the back, and dropping him in cold water, and taking a pussy willow and tickling him in the stomach. But nothing did any good. It looked like Mata had hypnotized him for life.

I guess it was about the third night, when I heard a loud crackling in the bushes again on the other side of the bayou. And then in the moonlight, showing between two

palmettos, I saw the head of a coyote. He motioned me not to make any noise.

"It's a friend," he whispered. "Let me come over."

And we put down the bridge log we always had ready and told him to come across.

"Don't trust him too much," warned the Brahma bull. "I've seen him around the outlaw camp a lot. I think he's very close to Mata."

The coyote hurried up and I saw right away I didn't like him a bit. He had a tricky, slippery face, and I watched him every minute.

"I know you're wondering why I came," he said, and his voice was smooth as syrup. "I don't blame you for being suspicious. But I can't stand staying back there an hour longer. I'm half coyote, half dog. My father worked as a watch dog in a big dry goods store in Tulsa, Oklahoma. It was all right when I was young, but now I'm older and wiser, and the dog part is taking over. It's bad enough that I want to chase Mata and the other coyotes. But now the dog part of me wants to chase the coyote part of myself. It's tearing me to pieces. I've decided to do like the Brahma bull. I've come to join you."

I took him to where Ironskin was sitting. I thought maybe Ironskin being a dog, even if he was hypnotized, could tell whether the coyote's story was true. Maybe if it was a coyote he'd growl, or if it was a dog he'd wag his tail. But all he did was look with his eyes all glassy and mumble a mountain song, something about Big Stone Gap.

And then I turned and saw a black shadow jumping off the log over the bayou.

"The coyote's a spy!" I shouted. And a second later I shouted again. "Look out! It's a tarantula!"

I ran to get a stick; but those big Western spiders are terribly fast. Before I could do

anything he'd bitten me in the paw, and he and the coyote were over the log and gone.

Where he'd bitten me burned like fire, but I knew I mustn't panic. A tarantula bite was almost as bad as a rattler for a raccoon; if I didn't keep cool, I'd be dead.

The poison began to run through my body, and I began to feel faint. "Don't let me lie down," I said to the others. "Keep me walking around. I'll stay alive as long as I'm moving."

And Judge Black and the rabbit took me under the arms and made me pace back and forth.

I began getting faint again, and everything around me began to shoot off balls of fire like Roman candles.

"I've heard that in Spain when a tarantula bites, everybody plays music and makes the bitten one dance," I heard Judge Black say. "Try to make him dance if we can."

The old frog started croaking a tune, and

Judge Black and the rabbit made me dance and keep time; I felt like a scarecrow trying to act in a show. All night they kept it up, and a couple of times I fell down; I couldn't go on any more. But each time they pulled me to my feet and made me start dancing again. And then it got daylight, and all of a sudden most of the pain was gone. There was only a bad swelling in my paw, and the snake doctor, flying past on his morning rounds, looked at me and said the worst was over.

"We'll have to watch every minute now for a new trick," I said. "These outlaws will stop at nothing."

We were sitting around next afternoon, when we noticed that the rattlers and the Gila Monsters on the other side of the bayou were gone, and then I thought I smelled smoke. And a minute later a wall of flames came sweeping toward the bayou.

"Down the burrow!" I shouted.

"They've set the marsh afire!"

I knew how they did it. Animals have done it plenty of times to people they don't like. They'd waited till the wind was right, and then snatched some burning pieces of kindling wood from the kitchen stove in the farmhouse at the edge of the cypress swamp, when the farmer's wife wasn't looking. I could tell you some stories about people that thought their house was burned down by lightning—but I guess I better not.

We jumped quick down the muskrat hole, dragging Ironskin with us. And a second later the fire crossed the bayou and raced over the island. We stayed down for hours, I guess, choking and sputtering, and hacking and coughing, moving farther and farther away, till we thought the fire was done. When we came out, it was night, and the ground was covered with ashes. Only here and there you could see little points of red where a bush or a log was still burning.

There wasn't a blade of grass left; every time you moved a paw it was covered with powder.

We had gone down in the burrow again, when we saw the mole and the muskrat come running; behind them was the skinny hound that'd followed Ironskin from the mountains.

The mole was shaking the way he'd done when we saw him at Catfish Bend. "We're finished," he panted. "We just heard some of the outlaws talking. Mata and the others say things are going too slow and there are too many of our animals still in the marshes. They're going to dig through the old bank of the river and let it come back here where it used to run. You and all the marsh animals 'll be drowned under ten feet of water . . . They're going to start digging at dawn."

6

For a few minutes the only sound was the rabbit's teeth rattling like when boys shake a bag of marbles.

"While there is life, there is hope," said Judge Black at last. "If only we could hear from J.C."

"J.C. is dead," groaned the frog. "Shot by a hunter. I saw it last night in a dream."

"I dreamed it, too," moaned the rabbit. "He was just coming to the Bend and a hunter behind a cypress shot him twice, right through the heart. He fell like a stone."

"It's a double dream," croaked the frog. "A double dream never fails."

The mountain hound came from the back

of the burrow now and started over to Ironskin.

"We found him wandering around in the muskrat tunnels and brought him here," said the mole. "He'd been lost for days."

The hound went up to Ironskin and whimpered. But Ironskin just stared at his old friend out of his stony eyes and growled and showed his teeth.

All night we talked and tried to think. And the hound lay down near Ironskin and began singing mountain songs, so soft you couldn't hear the words.

Daybreak came, and then I saw some ants crawling in for some crumbs we'd left on the floor.

I moved to the burrow entrance. "I'll be back by dark," I said to the others. "I think I have a plan."

I hurried through the tunnel and came out near a big anthill I'd seen under a dead cottonwood tree. Ants are supposed to be

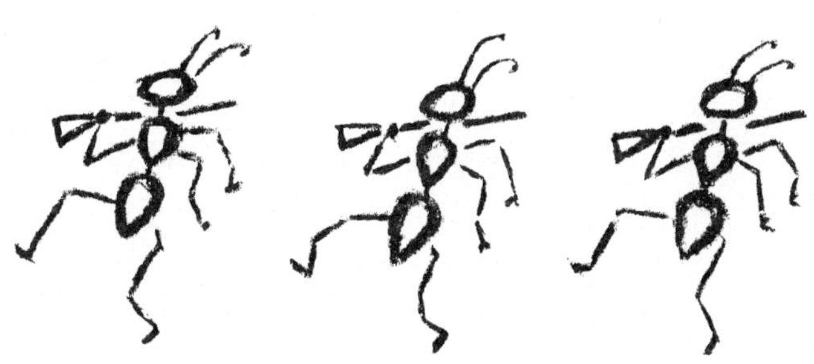

very wise; but I've always thought they don't have much sense.

A lot of big red ants were in front of the hill, going round and round in a circle. And I found which was the boss ant and marched around with him—he wouldn't stop—and I asked him what they were doing.

"We're getting ready for a war with those black ants over there," he said, and pointed with his feelers to some black ants I could see under a live oak tree, marching in a perfect square.

I asked him what they were fighting about.

He looked puzzled. "Don't be silly," he

answered. "Nobody ever asks that. But our fathers fought 'em and our grandfathers and their grandfathers before that. What was good enough for our grandfathers is good enough for us."

I marched around until my head was spinning, and I asked how going in a circle this way helped in the war.

"You don't know much about wars and armies," the boss ant said, looking disgusted. "It doesn't have to help. But the red ants here have gone in circles and the black ones in squares as far back as any ant can remember."

I told him about the outlaws and the flood, but he wasn't worried at all.

"These Westerners don't attack anything underground," he said. "And if the water comes we'll just climb up and settle in the trees. We've done it in plenty of floods before."

"Did you know they had armadillos with them?" I asked.

He was making the ants circle faster now, all the time calling out "Right, left, left, right." Ants don't march the same as people.

"What's an armadillo?" he asked, not paying much attention.

"It's a thing with a hard shell looks sort of like a turtle," I said. "Lives out in New Mexico and Texas. They can eat their weight in ants every seven minutes. Another name for them is anteater."

All the ants stopped marching like they'd had an electric shock. The boss red ant turned white. "Don't say that word, please," he asked me. "That's a word no ant ever mentions."

"There are maybe a couple of hundred of them," I said. "I saw them marching in yesterday. And I heard them say a lot more were on the way."

There were really only two, but I thought it was all right to use a little fox arithmetic.

Chapter Six

The boss ant turned to a messenger ant. "Rush over to the black ants and tell them to stop the war," he said. "And be sure to tell them the reason."

The ant raced off and a minute later the black ants stopped in their tracks.

"There isn't an ant anywhere won't give his life to help," the boss red ant said. "What do you want us to do?"

I told him fast, and hurried down to the river to find the alligators. There was a big one laying in the reeds, looking terribly skinny and miserable. And I was surprised to see it was Old Joe, the alligator who used to be at the Bend. Some ducks were flying around, and I knew he was waiting for one to make a mistake, so he could have a duck dinner.

I told him that, but he said it wasn't so. "I'm warning the ducks to stay away," he said. "There are a lot of bad alligators around."

I noticed he had something tied to his neck, and I looked closer and it was some kind of bird.

His eyes filled with tears. "It's a sea gull," he said. "I killed it one day when I hadn't eaten for a week. And then the marsh alligators took it from me because killing a sea gull's terrible bad luck. And they hung it around my neck, the way sailors used to do anybody that killed an albatross."

I asked him if he'd help.

"I'll try," he answered. "But I'm not the boss down here. Besides, the outlaws said we were water creatures and they had no water out in the desert, so there wasn't any reason to bother us."

"You wait till they find out the taste of alligator eggs," I said. "There won't be a young alligator left. The real reason they've let you alone so far is they think you're not worth bothering about. When I was their prisoner, I heard Mata say if an alligator got a toothache and had his teeth pulled, he'd be in terrible shape, because all his brains are in his mouth."

Old Joe gave a fearful bellow. "We'll get her for that," he said. And when I was a little way off, I heard the alligators bellowing all over.

I'd noticed when I was out before that the cypress swamp was full of wild razorback hogs, fierce fellows with terrible tusks curved like the sickles people use to cut grass. I hurried off to the farmhouse by the swamp, where I'd seen a lot of them eating the farmer's garbage.

I found the boss hog, an old fellow so fat his stomach scraped the ground when he walked. He was eating some coffee grounds, and he shoveled them down like a steamboat fireman shoveling coal.

"I ate some of these by accident," he said. "And now I've got the habit. If I don't have them first thing in the morning I get a splitting headache."

His little pig eyes looked worried. "Lately the grounds are getting fewer and fewer. They say it's because there's a new kind of coffee without any grounds. Every day my headaches seem to get worse."

I asked him if he'd help drive out the coyotes and the others, but he said he wasn't interested, just the same as the bears.

"The outlaws won't bother us razorbacks," he said. "We're really not wild animals at all. We're just ordinary pigs that have run a long time in the woods."

An old pig that was standing near gave an

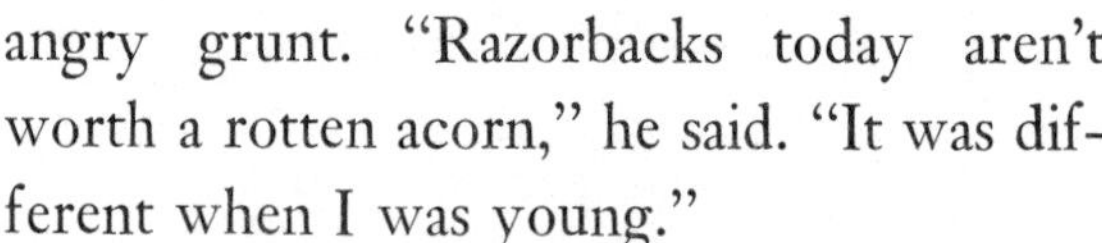

angry grunt. "Razorbacks today aren't worth a rotten acorn," he said. "It was different when I was young."

I waited a minute and then spoke very quietly. "There are a bunch of rattlesnakes with the outlaws," I said. "And more are coming in every minute."

The fat hog gave a jump and his pig eyes lighted. "Rattlers?" he grunted. "That's different. Why didn't you say so at once?" And then he looked sad. "I'm not the hog I used to be," he said. "Since I've been miss-

ing those coffee grounds, my headaches have made me weak as a cat."

"Come with me," I said. "I've something to show you." And we started across the marsh.

"I've got a lot saved up for those rattlers," the fat hog panted, and I noticed he limped on one of his front legs. "They gave me this knee for a souvenir. A knee's the only place on a pig a snake can hurt."

We came to a little place on the road along the river where the boatmen stopped to have a sandwich and coffee. And in back of it was a pile of coffee grounds where they'd been throwing them out for years; it was half as high as the building.

"This'll give you strength," I said. And I never thought a pig could be pretty. But when he saw those coffee grounds, his face was really beautiful. And when he left to round up the other hogs, I knew he wouldn't fail.

There was one more thing I was worried about. And then I saw some big crows hopping along, laughing their heads off like they were crazy, and I was sure I had the answer.

I went back to our burrow, and the mole and the muskrat were there with the others, waiting. And the hound was still laying by Ironskin's side, looking sad, and every once in a while he'd begin singing.

"The coyotes have started digging," the muskrat said. "And they've got a lot of muskrat zombies to help them. They expect to dig through by noon tomorrow."

I didn't waste any time. I turned to the muskrat and the mole. "Go out and tell every marsh animal you can find," I said. "We attack at first light in the morning."

I'd hardly gotten the words spoken when all of sudden Ironskin jumped to his feet.

"Fight it out!" he snarled. And then he broke down and cried. And everybody gave a big cheer. He was unhypnotized.

I guess it was the hound coming back and singing the mountain songs that had broken the spell.

He hurried off with the mole and the muskrat to talk to the marsh animals, and I went out in the woods and collected what I needed.

We didn't have a wink of sleep that night, getting everything ready. And at sunrise we started across the marsh, myself in the lead and Judge Black and Ironskin at my side. In back of us came the Brahma bull and the rabbit and the frog, with the mole and the muskrat running in and out of holes, scouting the way. And the farther we got, the more marsh and swamp animals came out to join us, otters and muskrats, and moles and ferrets, and raccoons and possums and mink. And back of them, with their horns all sharpened, were even a few marsh deer. After them came the water moccasins, and

the little pygmy rattlers from the cypress swamp had tiny coffins marked on their backs, and were so terrible they always said they were afraid of themselves. They all stretched out in a battle line to both ends of the sky.

Then the hogs came up, with the fat hog in the lead, and then the red ants and the black. And with them were some little red ants so thick they looked like a red carpet. I glanced around for Old Joe and the alligators, but he wasn't there, and I guessed they'd decided not to come.

We got close to the outlaws' camp and halted. And I called the muskrat and the mole and loaded them with some bundles of what I'd collected in the woods. I made them repeat what I'd told them to do so there'd be no mistake, and they disappeared down a hole.

And then I turned and faced our army, and everybody got so quiet, you could have heard a feather fall.

"Forward!" I called. And we started marching. And the battle began.

The first line of the outlaw camp was the prairie dogs, and we got through them fast. They were really nice little animals, and Ironskin had talked to them in the night. He'd told them how they were dogs like him, and how they'd be eaten when the coyotes didn't need them any more. And the prairie dogs said they knew it was true; they were only helping because the coyotes had scared them to death.

So now when we came near, they gave a couple of little barks, just in case the outlaws won, and ducked down into the prairie dog village.

The next line was the rattlers, and I gave the signal to the hogs, and they started racing toward the camp. The big snakes were coiled up, hissing and rattling, and it was enough to make your blood run cold. But in a second the fat hog was on his front knees, fighting a fearful looking snake, and the other hogs were on their knees like him. That's the way a hog fights a snake, so they can't bite him in that one spot. It looked like they were praying. A lot of new rattlers came out, and some of the hogs turned tail and ran. But the fat hog was wonderful and rushed around, grunting and squealing, and all of them came back in a hurry, and most of the snakes raced off. And Judge Black, looking terrible, came up with the moccasins and the pygmy rattlers and drove away any outlaw rattlers that were left.

We came to the third line, the Gila Monsters, and everybody stopped. The Gilas stood there, opening and shutting their mouths like bellows, breathing out their poison breath. It was so bad it was like a terrible wall nobody could get through alive. It looked like the battle was lost. And then I saw Old Joe waddling up, and behind him were all the marsh alligators. They charged into the Gilas, and the Gilas ran like chickens; the alligators were lizards the same as the Gilas, and they knew that to an alligator the Gila breath couldn't do any harm.

"Keep advancing!" I shouted to Ironskin. "A little more and we've won!"

And just then a shadow like a storm cloud came sweeping over the marsh toward us.

"Take cover!" I shouted. "It's the wild horses and the bulls!"

As many of us that could ducked down into holes or climbed up trees, but a lot couldn't get away. And the horses and the cattle came galloping down, with the wild mustang in the lead. And the noise of their hoofs was like the thundering of the sea. Twice more they charged this way, and then wheeled around and went back. And they formed a ring about the place where Mata and the other leaders stayed, and stood there neighing and roaring. And we went around picking up our animals that were hurt, and it made you very sad. We'd sent for a lot of snake doctors, but there weren't nearly enough to go around.

"It's the end," croaked the frog. "We'll never beat 'em. We're dead as mutton."

I waited till everybody had a little rest,

and then moved forward again to where the wild horses and the cattle were waiting. And they looked at us, wondering for a minute, and got ready to charge us again. I gave a signal to the red ant boss and out marched the little red ants that looked like a red carpet. And the horses and cattle saw them coming around their feet, and they began pawing and screaming.

"They're fire ants!" shouted the mustang. "Run to the river for your lives!"

They were the fire ants all right; when they get on you, they're like gasoline you've poured on yourself, and then you light a

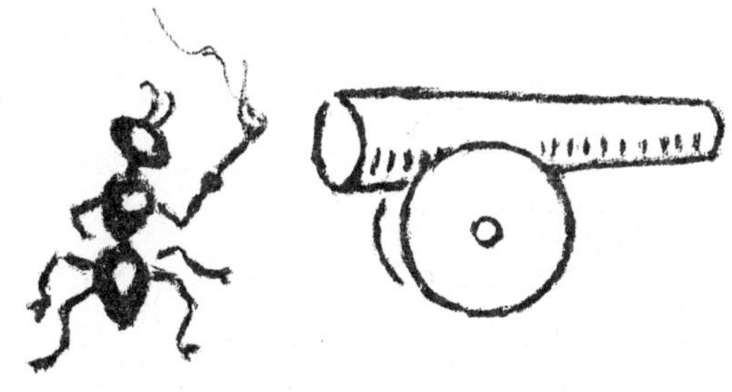

match. And the mustang and the horses and the bulls raced off every which way.

There was only one more line left, Mata and the coyotes. And they stood huddled together, with Mata and her husband out in front, grinding their teeth.

And then all of a sudden Mata began to laugh, and her husband and all the other coyotes looked at her, wondering what was the matter. And then her husband began laughing, too, and in a minute all the coyotes were laughing like they were crazy. And then they began rolling on the ground like cats that just found some catnip.

Course it was me that made them that way. I'd got the idea when I saw the crows laughing out in the swamp. The birds had been eating the crazy bean; that's the same as the loco weed out West, that a little while after they swallow it makes everybody silly. I'd gathered bundles of it where the birds had been and given them to the muskrat and the mole to put in the coyotes' breakfast.

We drove Mata and the coyotes down to the river, and drove away the ones cutting into the bank. Now that their leaders were gone nobody even tried to fight. We made them all cross the river and started them back toward the West. The last we saw of Mata and the coyotes, they were traveling into the setting sun, stopping every once in a while to roll on the ground, laughing their heads off. And that was the end of the Super Race.

We were still at the river when up the water we heard music. The old frog listened, and his gloomy face got all bright.

"It's the Indian Bayou Glee Club!" he croaked. "'They've come down from Catfish Bend!"

A minute later they came singing around the willows, and then we saw something else.

"It's J.C.!" I shouted. "He's arrived at last!"

Judge Black nodded. "Patience is its own

reward," he said. "Better late than never."

They came marching on, the little frogs in the lead singing Star Spangled Banner; behind them came J.C. and hundreds of swamp animals from back of New Orleans and Memphis and up as far as St. Louis. And there were a lot of house dogs and cats, even some little Pekinese and chihuahuas that had run away from their masters.

Course we made a big fuss over J.C., even if he had come too late to do any good. We camped right there by the Mississippi, and that night had a big celebration. And Ironskin and the mole and the muskrat thanked us for what we'd done, and everybody made fancy speeches. And Judge Black, like always, made the best speech, saying how pride goes before a fall, and

ending the way judges always do, "Crime doesn't pay."

And then J.C. stood up. "I sent word to the outlaws we were coming," he said. "That's why they didn't fight better. I'm glad I was able to save the day."

And everybody clapped, though they all knew it wasn't true. Everybody knew J.C.

After that the frog Glee Club sang Adeline, and Ironskin started getting jumpy. And then the hound dog sang Foggy Dew, and like always Ironskin broke down and cried. And then a big dog that had come down with the others ran up to Ironskin, and Ironskin's face all lighted.

"It's my uncle," Ironskin said. "From up in the Kentucky hills."

And they talked very quiet a minute, the way mountain people and animals do. And all of a sudden Ironskin's face shone like the golden moon that was just coming up over the river. And then he started crying again, but this time he was crying because he was glad.

"They've found out it wasn't me that killed the sheep," he snarled and sobbed. "It was an old dog that worked for a moonshiner up the creek. He confessed when he was dying. My uncle has come to tell me now I can go home again."

We traveled back to Catfish Bend. This time it was a long, hard trip, and we were all worn out before we started. We'd done

a fine job, but we'd been away a long time, and things at the Bend were in bad shape.

"Never again," I said to Judge Black and the others. "No matter who asks us to fix up their troubles, I'm not leaving. From now on I stay at home in the Bend."

And all the animals agreed.

"Peace has her victories no less than war," said Judge Black. "Wisdom is better than gold."

Half the time you never knew just what Judge Black meant, but it always sounded good.

The raccoon ended his story and we were still chatting when we saw a big otter coming down the river, swimming swift as a streak of lightning. The otter suddenly swung toward the shore, and jumping out of the water onto the bank, dashed dripping

wet to the raccoon. He stood there a minute, all out of breath, and then began talking, with the words popping out of his mouth so fast they sounded like firecrackers going off. Twice he sprayed me with water when he shook himself, and didn't even apologize. And I knew then he was really excited, because otters are usually very polite.

The raccoon listened, and then I could see he was as excited as the otter.

"I'm sorry," he told me. "I'll have to be excused. I have to round up Judge Black and the others. The animals back of Memphis are having terrible trouble with some strange animals they call wolverines have come down from the North. We've got to go there and help."